THE PRINCE AND THE DINOSAUR

Stephanie ♡

Stephanie Esirife

Once upon a time, there was a prince who loved to soak in his bath. He loved staying in his bath so much, that he ate his breakfast, lunch and dinner sitting in it.

What? Yes, he did!!!

He hardly ever came out of his bath to do anything. His teachers had to come and teach him while he was in it. Really?

His friends had to come and visit him there too and he only played water games with them.

Prince Eric even slept in the bath at nights. His father and mother begged him to come out of the bath, but he would not.

"He can never become the next king if he goes on like this," his father said, shaking his head.

His mother asked him sweetly, but still he would not get out.

"No princess will want to marry him if he does not get out of the bath," said his mother, wringing her hands.

They wondered what was going to happen to their son and the kingdom if he never came out of the bath.

As the prince grew older, he still did not come out of the bath to fight dragons eating their crops or to do any of the thing's princes were supposed to do around the palace.

All that he enjoyed doing was: eat, sleep play water games and listen to music. The next day: eat, sleep, play water games and listen to music...

Instead, he asked his father to build him a bigger bath as big as a pool. In it he learned to swim, dive and to stay under water for a very long time.

One day, a big bad dinosaur came to the kingdom where the prince lived.

With his big feet, he stomped on the fields destroying some of the crops.

The villagers screamed and ran away to hide.
The next day, the dinosaur came back and
did the same thing.

Horridly, someone dashed to tell the king, the prince's father.

Help!!!... They screamed terrifyingly. The king was very worried.

The King sent his senior soldier to but when he to saw how big the dinosaur was, he to ran as fast as he could screaming

Suddenly, a big feisty looking dinosaur grabbed and carried away a girl named Summer who was picking daisies in the field.

Now the king was really furious. He had to get back Summer. He asked his kings men what shall we do?

While some scratched his head in terror and fear, another said, "Your majesty, I...I...I... think this is a job for the prince."

Everyone had almost forgotten about the prince who never left the big bath. "Prince Eric must and should save our kingdom". Said the king firmly

The king hurried up to the bathroom where his son was lazily soaking in bubbled gum water.

"Hello, son," he said. "How are you today?" "I'm fine, Dad the prince replied. The water is so warm and nice. Do you want to come in?" asked prince Eric.

"No, son," the king said. Rolling his eyes "But we have a problem and need your help."

"Oh!" said the prince. His father had never bothered him or asked him to help before.

His father quickly told him about the big bad dinosaur and the things he had done.

"Then why don't you send the soldiers after him, Dad?" the prince asked as he splashed around at the same time eating his dinner. "I did, son. But they said he was so big and scary that they all ran away."

"Yes, son," the king told him, "because the dinosaur has taken the most stunning girl of our land and we must get her back." Not tomorrow or a day after but today by that, I mean right away!

When the prince heard this, he said, "Okay, Dad, I'll go".
Finally, the Prince came out of his comfort zone.

But the prince had stayed in the water for so long, they could not find any clothes to fit him. They were all too tight and his father's clothes were much too big.

Finally, the chief soldier found a suit of armour and a helmet. Though were a bit over sized, especially the helmet which kept sliding of his head, but there was nothing else suitable for prince Eric to wear.

"I have to do this, prince Eric whispered in fear to himself" I just have to do this. Its about time everyone sees me as a true prince and not just "the prince who loves to soak in the bath".

As the prince set out, they also gave him a sword. When the Prince got outside, the horse was patiently tapping its hove's.

When it was time to get on the horse, Prince Eric kept falling off but he was determined.

At last the Prince set out and everyone was worried. "He can barely balance on the horse," they wonder how he was going to fight the moody dinosaur. Tearing the entire village apart.

As soon as the prince was alone, he got down off the horse and charged to the river like lightning.

When he came to the river, he dove right in and swam across. It was just like being in his big pool at home. Then he went into the forest ?

Prince Eric found Summer locked inside a cottage in the woods.

The dinosaur was away looking for spices. So, the prince climbed in through a window and got her out.

Just then, they heard the moody dinosaur coming back and they started to run. The dinosaur chased after them. But because he was so big and they were so small, they kept slipping away, "woosh in, zoom out" from him until they came to the river. "Quick, come on and be brave," the prince told her, "and do exactly as I tell you."

"Quick, come on and be brave," the prince told Summer, "and do exactly as I tell you." Summer was a brave girl and she did what the prince said. "Now take a deep breath and hold it," he said.

As they heard the dinosaur crashing through the bushes, Prince Eric dove into the water with Summer. The river was wide and deep.

Down, down, down, Prince Eric and Summer went, holding their breath.

The dinosaur dove in after them. But Prince Eric was a good swimmer after spending all those years in the pool.

But the dinosaur did not know how to swim and he could not hold his breath for long and so he drowned.

The villagers cheered when Prince Eric and Summer returned to the palace. His parents were so proud of him.

His father now knew how good it was to be able to swim. His son wasn't just the prince that love to soak in the bath, but prince Eric was also brave by using his skills in the bath to save Summer and restore peace back to the whole village.

So, the king made a big pool in the palace yard for the prince who no longer stayed locked away inside. Instead, he taught all those who wanted to learn to swim.

Can you guess the first person who came for swimming lesson

Prince Eric's friends Or...?

Summer of course!

Do you think the prince misses soaking in his bath?